T0372143

CONTENTS

MEET BETTY AND HER FAMILY

Betty Yeti and her family moved from a cold mountain home to an apartment in the city. Mama Yeti, Betty and her twin brothers, Eddy and Freddy, are the only yetis in town. Getting used to a new place is hard. But it's especially hard when you're a yeti who isn't quite ready to stand out.

Mama

Eddy

Betty

Freddy

Chapter 1

MOVING DAY!

Two lorries parked outside the apartment building at the end of the street. Who was moving in?

Curious neighbours peeked out of their windows. All kinds of people lived in the building, but no one there had seen a family like this one.

Betty stepped out first, covered
in perfectly brushed white fur.
Betty was proud of her soft,
silky fur.

Next came Betty's twin brothers, Freddy and Eddy. After them, Mama Yeti stepped out.

The neighbours gasped! They did not expect a family of yetis!

The Yetis had come from
a snowy, faraway mountain.
They had never lived around
people before.

Betty, for one, thought people were strange. "They are so small," Betty said to Mama. "And they have so little fur."

"Creatures come in all shapes and sizes," said Mama.

Chapter 2

A SURPRISE VISIT

Finally, the Yetis had carried in every box. Eddy took his gaming system to the boys' room. Freddy took his baseball bat. Betty picked up her box of soft toys.

Suddenly, there was a knock on the door. Betty froze. She was afraid to meet a human!

Betty's heart raced! She hid behind a stack of boxes. Mama Yeti opened the door. A smiling man and a girl stood there.

"Welcome to the building," said the man. "I'm Dan Romano. This is my daughter, Cecilia. We've brought you my famous spaghetti."

"Thank you!" said Mama.
"What a nice surprise."

Betty's mind raced. What
would she say to them? And what
was spaghetti? Betty had to admit,
it smelled good. Her tummy
grumbled. Everyone heard it!

"Sounds like someone is hungry!" said Mr Romano. He peeked over at Betty.

Chapter 3

TRYING SOMETHING NEW

"Moving has made us hungry," said Mama. "Betty, would you like to try some spaghetti?"

"Okay," said Betty with a shy smile.

She looked at the strange new food. It looked a bit like her favourite meal, snowball surprise – balled up snow with berries.

Betty stuck a fork into a red, gooey meatball. Sauce dripped all the way to her mouth. When Betty tasted it, she made a face.

Spaghetti tasted NOTHING like snowball surprise. Then Betty saw her fur. It was a mess!

Betty ran to her room.

"I HATE spaghetti!" she cried.

Chapter 4

CECILIA'S SURPRISE

A few minutes later, someone knocked on Betty's door.

"Hello?" Cecilia Romano poked her head into Betty's room.

"I'm sorry our spaghetti upset you," said Cecilia. "We thought you would like it."

"No, I'm sorry," said Betty.
"Spaghetti just wasn't what
I was expecting."

"What were you expecting?"
asked Cecilia.

Betty's eyes lit up as she told
Cecilia about snowball surprise.

"That sounds yummy," said Cecilia.

"You can come over when we make it," said Betty.

"Yes, please!" said Cecilia with a giggle.

"Maybe spaghetti isn't so bad," Betty said. "Everything is just new and different here. It's . . . scary."

Cecilia sat by Betty. "I know what you mean," she said. "When we moved here, I was scared too. Do you know what made it better?"

"What?" asked Betty.

"When I made friends," said Cecilia.

"Do you think I'll make a friend here?" asked Betty.

"I hope you already have," said Cecilia, smiling.

Betty smiled back. "I'm starting to feel better already," she said.

Glossary

apartment home that has its own rooms and front door, but shares outside walls and a roof with other apartments; many neighbours share an apartment building

curious eager to explore and learn about new things, like yetis and new tasty treats

gasp take a sudden breath out of excitement

silky smooth and glossy, like silk and yeti fur

yeti large, furry ape-like creature that may or may not exist in cold, faraway places

Talk about it

1. Betty was nervous about moving to a new place. Have you ever moved to a new place? How did you feel about it? Were you nervous about anything?

2. Betty ran to her room after she tried the spaghetti. Why do you think she did that? What do you think she was feeling?

3. Have you ever tried a new food that didn't taste like you expected it to? What was it? How did you handle it?

Write about it

1. Betty's family travelled from a faraway mountain home to a big apartment in the city. Draw a map following their journey. Imagine the places they saw on their trip.

2. Betty loves her mum's recipe for snowball surprise. How do you think Mama Yeti makes it? Create a recipe for how you would make snowball surprise. Are there any special recipes that you love? You can write out that recipe too.

3. At the end of the story, Betty feels like she has made a friend. Write about a time you made a friend.

About the author

Mandy R Marx is a writer and editor. She lives in a chilly town in Minnesota, USA, with her husband, daughter and a white, silky haired pup. She has a curious mind and stays on the lookout for yetis. In her spare time, Mandy enjoys singing, laughing with friends and family and walking her pup through what she suspects is a magical forest.

About the illustrator

María Antonella Fant is a visual designer, children's book illustrator and concept artist. Her illustrations reflect her childish, restless and curious personality, taking inspiration from animated cartoons and children's books from her childhood. María enjoys the way a child thinks, drawing like them and for them. María was born, and currently lives, in Argentina.